D1508150

THE SECRET EXPLORERS
AND THE MOON MISSION

CONTENTS

Chapter One
THE FLYING BEAGLE

Roshni's heart filled with joy as she gazed at the stars in the sky above her backyard. She thought she could name each one. But she also knew there were thousands more that weren't visible because of light pollution from her busy city of New Delhi, in India.

Tonight, she'd set up her telescope and trained it on the moon. Roshni laid a large circular sheet of paper on a folding table and put her eye to the telescope.

"Wow! The moon looks huge tonight—much bigger than a usual full moon," she murmured. Roshni knew this was because the moon was at the point in its orbit when it was closest to Earth. Most people called it a supermoon, but Roshni was an astronomer, and she preferred the technical term, "perigee-syzygy." She loved those words, even though they were difficult to say. She said them aloud now. "Perigee-sigizee!" She giggled. Wrong again! But no one could hear except the nighttime creatures scuttling and crawling among the lush garden plants.

Roshni settled down to study the moon's landscape, so she could add details to the map she was drawing. She focused on a wide flat area. It was one of the moon's maria, which Roshni knew was Latin for seas. A mare was a sea formed by ancient volcanoes, rather than water.

She added it to her moon map, wondering what it would be like to be there.

"Meow!" Roshni's striped little cat, Luna, called from a branch of one of her mom's mango trees. As Roshni looked up, she noticed a strange light glowing on the high garden wall behind Luna.

She ran to it, and caught her breath. Yes! The light was the symbol of a compass, with pointers marked N, E, S and W. She touched the matching badge on her T-shirt, and shivered with excitement.

Roshni was one of a group of eight children from different parts of the world. Each was a specialist in a particular subject, and they used their expertise to solve difficult problems. Together, they were the Secret Explorers, and Roshni was their Space expert. The glowing compass meant they had an exciting new mission!

As she stepped forward, the wall seemed to ripple and a shiny steel door appeared around the compass symbol.

"Here I go," Roshni breathed. She opened the door and stepped into brilliant white light.

As the light faded, she found herself in the Secret Explorers' headquarters—the Exploration Station!

"Roshni, here!" she called, but there was no reply. She was the first to arrive. The computers, which were ranged against a gleaming black stone wall, were silent. Roshni wandered past the displays of amazing objects that the Explorers had collected on their missions, and flopped into a squishy armchair. There was a huge map of the world in the center of the floor, but Roshni preferred to lean back and look upward. On the ceiling was a live image of the Milky Way—the galaxy that is home to the Earth's solar system. That was where Roshni's heart belonged—in space!

The door opened and a tall girl with grass-stained knees came in. She grinned and saluted. "Leah here!" She was the Biology Explorer.

Next was the Geology Explorer. "Cheng here!" he said, and he was almost sent flying by the Engineering Explorer, who followed close behind.

"Kiki here!" she said. "Sorry, Cheng!"

Roshni smiled. Kiki had obviously been busy—her denim shorts had oil stains all over them.

Another boy arrived next. "Gustavo here!" he announced as he peeled off a pair of white gloves. "I've just been dusting an ancient statue," he explained. Gustavo was the History Explorer.

"Connor here!" said the group's Marine Explorer. He was followed by Tamiko, who wore her favorite Stegosaurus barrette. She was the Dinosaur Explorer.

The Rainforest Explorer came in last. "Ollie here!" he said, pulling off his bucket hat.

The Secret Explorers formed a circle around the floor map.

"Where will our mission be?" Gustavo said excitedly. "Or when? The sixteenth century?"

"Maybe in the ocean!" said Connor.

"A Jurassic forest?" Tamiko said hopefully.

"Stopping a gang of thieves from stealing rare bird eggs?" suggested Leah.

They held their breath as the world map changed. Blue seas, yellow deserts, and vivid green forested areas turned gray and merged together. Mountain ranges appeared, and wide craters dotted the land.

"They could be quarries," Cheng said. "Or the mouths of volcanoes."

"I don't think so," said Tamiko. "In fact, I don't think the map looks like anywhere on Earth."

"That's because it isn't," Roshni burst out. Her voice trembled with excitement. "It's a map of the moon!"

A glowing pinpoint appeared on a circular area. It grew into a beam of light that projected up from the map and opened into a screen.

Heads tipped to one side, and eyes squinted at the picture. It showed some sort of vehicle inside a crater.

"Roshni?" said Gustavo. "What's that?"

She knelt to look closer. "It's a lunar rover," she said. "There are no seats, so it's not meant for astronauts. It's a robotic rover."

Kiki grinned. "An astrobot!"

"Exactly," said Roshni. She sat back on her heels. "It's designed to rove across the moon's surface collecting samples and data," she explained. "But this one looks as if it's stuck in a crater. The sides must be too steep for it to get out."

"That must be our mission," said Ollie. "We need to rescue that lunar rover so it can get back to work."

"So who will the Exploration Station choose for the mission?" Leah wondered.

Roshni crossed her fingers for luck, thinking, *let it be me, oh let it be me...*

"It's you!" cried Connor. He pointed at Roshni's compass badge. It had lit up!

She leapt to her feet. "Who's coming with me?"

Cheng's badge lit up, too. He punched the air. "It's me!" he said. "Oh my gosh! I'm

going to see lunar rocks!"

Tamiko laughed. "That's why you were chosen," she said. "The Exploration Station always picks the right Explorers for our missions. The rest of us will be at our computers ready to help if you need us!"

"Thanks, Tamiko," said Roshni, hopping from one leg to the other. She couldn't wait to leave. "Kiki, you're nearest—press the button!"

Kiki straightened her glasses and pressed a red button on the wall.

A hatch opened in the floor and up rose what looked like an old go-kart. Its paint was flaking and its wheels were rusty and bent. It didn't look as if it could go anywhere, but the Secret Explorers knew differently.

This battered vehicle was the Beagle. It was named after the ship that carried the great scientist and explorer, Charles Darwin, on his adventures around the world. The Explorers' Beagle had been on many adventures, too—on land, sea, and air!

Roshni and Cheng clambered into the two seats. It was a tight fit, but they knew that wouldn't matter. Roshni gripped the dented steering wheel. Everyone said, "Good luck!" and she pressed the "GO" button. Bright white lights surrounded the Beagle, and she felt it begin to transform. Roshni found her hands were clutching thin air. The steering wheel had disappeared.

Before she had time to wonder what was happening, the light faded. Now they were surrounded by screens, control panels, and closed compartments.

Roshni squealed in delight as a roof slid into place. "The Beagle's turned into a spacecraft!" She tried to sit up, but found seat belts held her firmly on a couch.

BEEP! BEEP! went the Beagle, as if to say hello.

"Woah," Cheng said in a low voice, as he looked through a window. "There's an enormous... thing in front."

Roshni realized what the enormous thing was. "It's the moon, Cheng. The moon! I can see craters and mountains!"

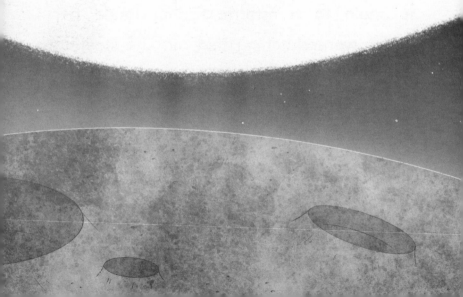

"And it seems to be growing larger," Cheng said in awe. "You know what that means..."

Roshni did! "It means we're flying toward it," she said, thrilled. "The Beagle's turned into a lunar module—and we're going to land on the moon!"

Chapter Two
EMERGENCY!

Roshni checked out the Beagle's controls and equipment, and soon realized it was pretty old-fashioned. "It's like the Eagle on the Apollo 11 mission," she told Cheng.

He looked puzzled. "An eagle?"

"Not an eagle," said Roshni. "The Eagle—the lunar module that made the very first moon landing, back in 1969."

"Cool!" said Cheng. "So that means—oh, what was his name? Neil Armstrong, that's it. The first person ever to walk on the moon was in a lunar module exactly like this?"

Roshni peered closely at various switches. "Hmm, not exactly like this," she said. "The Beagle has a few controls of its own."

Cheng grinned. "I'm sure they'll be perfect for this mission."

BEEP!

Roshni laughed. "The Beagle agrees!"

A screen to the right burst into life. Written at the top was, "Your mission."

Cheng read it out. "The robotic lunar rover you were shown in the Exploration Station is in trouble on the far side of the moon. Your mission is to rescue it and help it continue to search for a location for a new radio telescope."

"That will be a great place for it," said Roshni. "The far side always faces away from Earth, so the telescope won't have any radio interference from our planet."

Cheng looked blank. "What does a radio telescope do?" he asked.

Roshni explained that the telescope would gather weak radio signals from stars and galaxies. "Scientists use an amplifier to make the signals clearer, so they can study them," she said.

"What for?" asked Cheng.

"To help them learn about stars' movements

and how they were formed, and about clouds of gases, and they listen for alien signals..." Roshni began.

CLICK. CLICK-CLICK-CLICKETY-CLICK.

The Beagle's automatic landing controls were taking the module lower, so it was almost skimming the moon's surface.

"That's a relief," Roshni said. "I've been worrying about landing. The astronauts were at the controls when they landed. But it looks as if the Beagle's got it all covered." She checked their position on the map screen. "Look," she cried, bubbling with delight. "We're heading for the far side of the moon!"

Cheng opened his mouth to reply, but the Beagle suddenly shuddered and rocked.

BEEP! BE-BE-BEEP! BEEPBEEPBEEP!

"The Beagle sounds panicky!" Cheng cried.

"I think we've hit something." Roshni's voice quavered. She pointed to one of the screens that showed different views from the module. "There! In the rear screen. See that huge rock behind us? We must have clipped it. I hope the Beagle's not damaged."

BEEBEEBEEBEEBEEBEEBEEEEEEEEP!

"That definitely does sound panicky," Roshni groaned. "I don't think we're going to make it all the way to the far side on the moon..."

A red light came on above the screen, and the words "EMERGENCY" flashed on and off.

"Hold tight, Cheng!" Roshni cried, undoing her straps. "The far side will have to wait—we need to land right now!" She pulled herself to the controls, feeling as if she'd float away if she didn't hold on to something. "I'm worried we might end up in a deep crater. I'm going to try to land the Beagle myself."

There was a quiet **BEEP!**

"The Beagle sounds relieved," said Cheng. "I wish I was!"

Roshni pulled the lever marked "Manual Control" and, with helpful beeps from the Beagle—soft ones for "you're doing okay," and loud ones for "don't touch that"—she began to steady the module.

"Look for a suitable landing place," she told Cheng. "I'm having a struggle staying level. The Beagle seems to be lopsided. It's hard to keep it upright, especially when I feel so floaty that I can't be sure I'm upright myself! The moon's low gravity is going to take some getting used to."

Cheng pointed ahead and slightly to the left. "There—will that work?"

Roshni saw a wide plain in front of them. It was a grayish-blue color, and appeared fairly flat.

"Looks good, Cheng," she said. "Bring up the map."

As the screen filled, she saw that they were heading straight toward the Sea of Tranquillity.

"You couldn't have found a better place to land," she told Cheng. "This is where the Eagle landed in 1969."

"Wow!" Cheng said, gazing out in awe. "So this is where humans first walked on the moon."

Roshni nodded. "Let's hope we aren't the first humans to crash on the moon," she said grimly.

The landing was bumpy, and Roshni found it hard to keep control.

"I'm glad I stayed strapped in my couch," said Cheng. "Oof! Oof! Oof!" he added, as they bounced three times. A moment later, with a relieved sounding **BEEP**, the Beagle was still. Everything seemed stable, although it was tilted slightly to one side.

Roshni pushed away from the controls and pulled herself down onto her couch. She took a deep, shaky breath.

Cheng raised his hand. "That was an awesome landing. Good job!" he said.

Roshni high-fived him. "We made it," she said. "The Beagle has landed!"

Chapter Three
MOON WALKING

The two Explorers had helped each other into their space suits and helmets. Roshni knew they would give her and Cheng everything they needed to stay alive on the moon—oxygen to breathe, insulation to keep warm, and a tinted visor to protect their eyes from the sun. She found that the extra weight also meant she didn't float whenever she moved, and she didn't have to pull herself around. Cheng seemed to like kicking off from the floor and floating upward, though!

Roshni spoke clearly and carefully in a loud voice. "Can... you... hear... me?"

Cheng giggled. "Loud and clear, just as if you were inside my helmet bellowing in my ear!"

"Sorry!" Roshni laughed. "It's a great communication system, isn't it?" She moved to an open hatch, where a ladder led down to the moon's surface. Cheng stood behind her.

Roshni was so excited that she had to take several deep breaths to calm herself down. This was a dream come true. She was actually going to set foot on the gray, dusty surface of the moon.

She stepped down carefully, holding tight to the ladder's handrails. She didn't want to fall and damage her spacesuit. Roshni didn't like to think what would happen to her if all the air was sucked out of it.

"This must be how Neil Armstrong felt," she heard Cheng say.

"And Buzz Aldrin," said Roshni, taking another step. "Two astronauts landed in the Eagle. Actually, there was a third man on the Apollo 11 flight. Michael Collins had to stay in the command module and wait for the Eagle to return."

"That must have been hard," said Cheng, "being so close and not being able to walk on the moon."

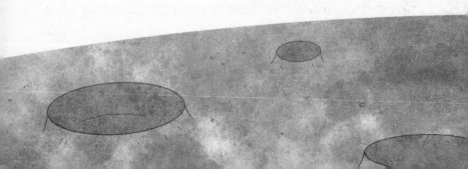

Roshni was trembling with excitement. She reached the last rung of the ladder, and hoped her shaky legs would hold her up.

"Here I go," she said, and put one foot on the ground. "Roshni is—on the moon!"

She put her other foot down and took a step forward so Cheng could follow. "Wow!" she said. "It feels weird—like I could take off!" She turned to see Cheng's feet slipping off the steps.

"Woah! I moved too fast!" he said, grasping the handrails with his thickly gloved hands.

Roshni reached out a steadying arm, and soon they stood side by side.

"That felt strange," said Cheng. "In fact, I feel a bit odd right now, even though I'm on the ground."

"That's because the gravity's so low. It's only about a sixth of Earth's gravity, so walking won't be normal," Roshni said. "Let's experiment—and be careful, because the dust is a bit slippery."

Within a short while, they were moving around without fearing they'd fall down or take off.

"Look at me," cried Cheng, doing long jumps with his feet together.

Roshni laughed. "You're a kangaroo!"

She took long, loping strides, feeling she was gliding over the ground for seconds at a time. "This is amazing!"

Slowing herself down, Roshni turned to see what Cheng was doing. She gasped. "Oh! Oh, Cheng, look!"

In the dark sky was a magical, majestic view of planet Earth. It was breathtaking, like a blue marble, swirled with white.

She heard Cheng's long, low "Wooooowww!"

Roshni stared at it silently. She was grateful for the lack of light pollution here on the moon. The awesome sight was beyond her dreams. "I feel like the luckiest person in the galaxy," she said quietly.

"Earth's so far away," Cheng said in an awed voice.

"About 240,000 miles," said Roshni. "That's quite close, really. When the moon is at its farthest point away from Earth—that's known as 'lunar apogee'—you'd have to travel about 252,000 miles to—"

Cheng broke in. "Oh, no!" he said, pointing to the Beagle. Roshni turned to look too. It really was lopsided.

"Something's wrong with one of the legs," Cheng said. "It must have gotten damaged when we hit that big rock."

Roshni's heart sank. They would never be able to continue their journey to the far side of the moon with the Beagle in that state.

"Now what?" Cheng asked anxiously. "We can't exactly call for a rescue pickup." He looked at Roshni. "The Exploration Station should have sent Kiki—she'd know what to do."

Roshni wanted to give him a hug, but it was impossible in their bulky space suits. "You were chosen for a reason," she said. "We don't know what it is yet—but we will." She went to the ladder. "At least we know who to ask for help."

Soon they were back on board, with Cheng turning a dial on the control panel. "Beagle to Exploration Station," he said. "Beagle to Exploration Station..."

Roshni waited anxiously. "The Explorers usually respond quickly," she said.

"I know," said Cheng, "but we're a long way away. It will be OK, Roshni."

"...and Roper's sent it down the wing—it's picked up by Banchero—he passes..."

Roshni perked up when she realized the Beagle had tuned in to a snatch of soccer commentary. It was eerie being on the moon and hearing bits of radio shows from Earth. Music, stand-up comedy, talk shows— all jumbled together.

"Try again," she urged.

Cheng fiddled with the dial. "Beagle to Exploration Station..."

Suddenly, they heard Connor's voice! "Beagle, are you receiving? Exploration Station to Beagle..."

Roshni quickly pressed a button to lock on to the signal. The screen woke up, and there were six Secret Explorers' faces smiling at them. They fired questions at Roshni and Cheng.

"Have you landed?"

"What's it like?"

"What can you see?"

Roshni held up a hand. "Whoa! Questions later. We need help."

She explained about the Beagle's damaged leg. Everyone moved aside so Engineer Kiki could speak.

She drew a rough sketch on paper and held it up for Roshni and Cheng to see. "It's basically a joint," she explained, "a bit like your knee, and this is the part you need. You'll also need a wrench, some bolts, a screwdriver, duct tape... lots of duct tape..."

"Slowly!" said Cheng. "I'm writing this down." When he'd finished, he looked back at Kiki. "Is that everything?"

"Well, yes," said Kiki, looking worried. "You can fix the leg all right, but there's a problem."

"I know," said Cheng. "Where are we going to find a spare joint on the moon?"

Almost before he'd finished speaking, the answer popped into Roshni's head.

She felt a huge smile spread across her face.
"Don't worry," she said. "I know where!"

Chapter Four
SPACE JUNK

Roshni clambered down the Beagle's ladder and set off. She covered the ground easily with long, loping strides.

"This is fantastic!" cried Cheng as he followed her across the moon's dusty surface. "I feel so light, I could float off into space!"

Roshni laughed. "Lucky for you there's enough gravity to keep us down," she said.

"I suppose you know where we're going," said Cheng.

"Not really," she said. "I only know that the astronauts left lots of equipment behind—even old lunar modules." She bounced gently to a stop and gazed around. "We just need to find them."

Cheng paused, too, then he leaned over as far as he could in his bulky space suit. He peered at rocks around his feet. "Basalts!" he cried.

"Bless you!" said Roshni.

Cheng laughed. "That wasn't a sneeze!"

Roshni giggled. "Good—you don't want one of those inside your helmet!"

"I was telling you what these rocks are called," said Cheng. "They're made from cooled lava." He knelt down carefully, and picked one up. It was the size of a large lump of coal, but gray rather than black, and it was peppered with tiny holes. He reached around to put it in the backpack that was built into his space suit. Impossible!

Roshni saw Cheng struggle to get off his knees. She kangaroo-hopped over and helped him up.

"Whew," he said. "That's not easy to do in a space suit. Can I put this rock in your backpack?"

"You want me to carry a heavy lump of rock?" she asked in surprise.

"One-sixth gravity, you said," he reminded her. "It will feel light."

Roshni smiled. "Of course," she said, turning her back.

She grinned slyly. "I do believe that's a bag of astronaut poop by your foot!"

"Whaaat?" Cheng bobbed aside. "Yuck!"

"Watch where you walk," said Roshni. "Those poop bags might be important. You never know—future scientists could study it to see how human microbes survive on the moon. Come on, let's check out the machinery and try to find the joint replacement."

While they searched, Roshni told Cheng about other things astronauts had left on the moon, like a gold olive branch that was a symbol of peace, a family photo, some golf balls, and a single feather they'd used in a gravity experiment.

Cheng picked up a small broom like the one Roshni's mom used to sweep the stairs. "What would an alien make of this?" he asked. "I wish I'd brought something that I could leave for aliens to wonder about."

Roshni pointed behind him. "You have—look!"

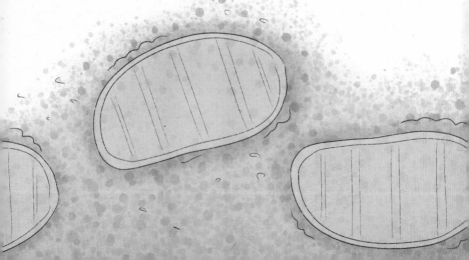

Cheng turned. "My footprints! But they're in dust," he said. "They won't last long."

"They will," said Roshni, heading toward a heap of machinery. "The moon has no atmosphere, so there's no wind to blow the dust away. Look around—you'll see footprints of astronauts who've been here before. Oh my goodness!"

Cheng bounded across to her. "What's up? What's wrong?"

"Nothing," said Roshni. "Something's right. Extremely right! I've found a part we can use to repair the Beagle's leg!"

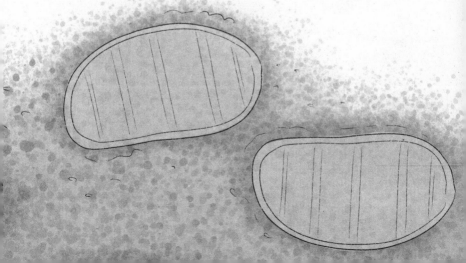

Back at the Beagle, Cheng and Roshni followed Kiki's excellent instructions, and soon finished repairing the broken joint.

They kangaroo-hopped toward each other and bounced upward for a low-gravity high-five, saying, "We did it!"

"It's lucky everything seems so much lighter on the moon," said Cheng. "Changing that heavy joint was a lot easier than it would have been on Earth."

They packed their tools away and climbed on board. Once they'd drawn the ladder up and taken off their space suits, they pulled themselves down onto their couches and strapped in.

"Away we go!" said Roshni, as the Beagle began the liftoff process, rising vertically from the moon's surface.

Roshni noticed that Cheng was frowning slightly. Something was bothering him. "What's up?" she asked.

"I'm wondering if we've got enough fuel

to complete our mission," he said. "You told me how the astronauts only have enough to get them back to their command module. Suppose we run out? Suppose next time we can't lift off and escape from the moon's gravity? Suppose—"

"Don't worry," Roshni interrupted, as she adjusted the cooling system, "I'm sure the Beagle has everything under control."

BEEP BEEP BEEP.

Cheng laughed. "I'm sure the Beagle just said, "Of course I do!""

CLICK. CLICK-CLICKETY-CLICK, went the automatic controls, as the Beagle changed direction and leveled off, flying above the rocky ground.

"Here we go," said Roshni. She was scarcely able to believe it. "We're off to the far side of the moon!"

Chapter Five
DANGER—BALLS IN THE AIR!

"It beats me how a spacecraft as small as the Eagle flew to the moon and back, even with the command module," said Cheng. "How did it carry enough fuel for such a long journey?"

Roshni gazed through the window as they flew above the moon's surface. "There was more to the Apollo 11 mission than the Eagle," she said. "The rocket was made up of sections. The huge bottom part that blasted them into space was called Saturn V. On top of that was Columbia, which carried the service module with things like oxygen, water and fuel."

"Where were the astronauts?" Cheng wondered.

"In the other part of Columbia—the command module. That was the only part that returned to Earth."

"So when Columbia reached the moon, Armstrong and Aldrin got into the Eagle and flew down to the surface?" Cheng asked.

Roshni nodded. "Michael Collins orbited the moon in Columbia until it was time for the Eagle to fly back. Once the astronauts were safely in the command module, they let the Eagle go. No one's quite sure where it is."

"Aha!" said Cheng. "I think I know why they ditched it. Was it because it wasn't needed anymore, and it was unnecessary weight?" He patted the control panel. "Don't worry, Beagle. We won't ditch you."

BEEEP.

"In a while." Roshni said slowly, "we'll actually be on the far side of the moon." A thrill seemed to travel from her toes to the top of her head.

"I've heard people talk about the dark side of the moon before," said Cheng. "Is it the same thing?"

"Yes, that's right," said Roshni. she explained that even though it's sometimes called the dark side, the far side of the moon actually gets two weeks of sunlight at a time, the same as the side that always faces Earth. "People call it 'dark' because we don't know much about it, not because it doesn't get any sunlight," she added.

Cheng thought for a moment. "So will it be light when we get there?"

Roshni checked the screens. "By my calculations, we'll arrive just before dawn. It will still be dark."

"So we'll just wait for sunrise, then start searching—is that right?" he asked.

She grinned. "Definitely. Are you hungry?"

"Yes!" said Cheng. "Everything's been so exciting that I haven't thought about food. I could do a disappearing trick with a bowl of fries!"

Roshni laughed. "I won't find anything like that!" She took a pouch from a compartment and passed it to him.

"What's this?" he said. "There's no label."

"Open it," said Roshni.

He opened the pouch. "Tortillas!" he said. "I could make a taco if I had anything to put in it. I'd rather have a sandwich than an empty taco."

"Astronauts don't have bread because it goes bad quickly and makes crumbs," Roshni said. "If crumbs got into a spacecraft's working parts, they'd really mess things up."

BEEPBEEPBEEEEEEP! went the Beagle, making them laugh.

"Here, have an empty taco," Cheng said. "I hope there's something else to eat."

Roshni explored the food compartment. "Aha!" she said, and held up a jar of peanut butter and one of raspberry jam.

"Yay!" said Cheng. He held the jars while Roshni spread the peanut butter on the tortillas, and added raspberry jam.

"Two tacos!" she said proudly.

When they'd polished them off, Roshni took out another pouch from a cold compartment. "I wish these pouches had labels," she said, opening it. Inside were some pale cubes. She put one in her mouth. "Ice cream!" she said in surprise. "It's been freeze-dried. I remember reading that the Apollo 11 astronauts ate this. Here, try some."

Cheng took the pouch from her and tipped it up over his open hand. Nothing happened, so he shook it. Five or six cubes drifted out and hung in the air. He caught and ate most of them but, as he grabbed at the last one, he accidentally knocked it away.

"Get it!" cried Roshni. "It could get stuck in the Beagle's electronics!"

Cheng unclipped his seat belt and jumped up, grabbing the ice cream cube.

Roshni laughed at his expression as he shot upward and bumped his head on the ceiling. "You forgot how much lighter you'll feel in the moon's low gravity!"

He grinned. "This gravity's fantastic!" he said. "Imagine doing the high jump on the moon—or pole vaulting!"

Roshni pulled him back onto his couch. "Strap in," she said. "You'll be bouncing off the walls otherwise!"

Cheng sat back and looked through the window. "The scenery's a bit samey, isn't it?" he said. "Anything else to eat?"

Roshni found another pouch. "This feels soft and there's a built-in tube thingy so you can squirt what's inside into your mouth. I'll try it." She giggled. "Here goes."

As she squeezed the pouch, the food squidged into her mouth. She pinched the tube shut. "Yum! Apple pie," she said. "The Beagle is so smart. The first astronauts wouldn't have had anything like this. Their meals were dried and they had to add water to rehydrate them. Want one, Cheng?"

"Yes, please," he said eagerly.

With her free hand, Roshni found another pouch. "This feels the same," she said, passing it to Cheng. "Enjoy!"

BEEEEEP!

She wondered why the Beagle was beeping. Was it telling her something?

Cheng put his mouth to the tube, but he squeezed too hard. He struggled not to splutter as his mouth filled up. He pinched the tube shut and looked at Roshni with bulging cheeks.

"Swallow!" she cried. "Don't let any leak out! Remember the Beagle's electronics!"

Cheng managed to get the food down. "Yuck!" he said. "Cold mushroom soup!"

BIPBIPBIPBIPBIPBIPBIP!

Roshni grinned. "The Beagle's laughing!"

"Yeah, that beep when you gave me the pouch was probably a warning," said Cheng.

"Let's see," said Roshni, taking out another one.

BEEP! BEEP!

"That's it," said Cheng. "One beep for don't-give-that-to-Cheng, and two beeps for he'll-like-it."

"You hope!" Roshni giggled, passing the pouch to him.

This time, he gave her a thumbs-up. "Chocolate mousse!" he said. "But it's not that good. Actually, none of this food tastes of much at all."

"You need to be able to smell food to taste it properly," Roshni said. "The low gravity means the smell isn't reaching our noses. And there's another reason astronauts don't have a very good sense of smell—without enough gravity, some fluids block their noses instead of flowing around their bodies, like when we have colds."

"Talking of fluids," said Cheng, "I need a drink."

BEEP.

A light flashed on a compartment. Inside were two pouches marked "Drink mix." They were filled with powder, and above them was a short nozzle. Roshni put the tube of one pouch to the nozzle, and water squirted inside. She gave it to Cheng. "The Apollo 11 astronauts drank this!" she told him.

"Really?" he said. "It's just a bunch of powder with water on top."

"Shake it, but keep the tube pressed shut until you're ready to drink," she warned. "If you squeeze the pouch at the wrong time we'll have sticky liquid everywhere. You know what that does to computer keyboards. Imagine what it would do to the Beagle."

There was a short, sharp *BIP!*

Roshni laughed. "Don't worry, Beagle," she said. "We wouldn't make a silly mistake like that!"

As they gulped their orange drinks, Cheng turned to Roshni and crossed his eyes. She spluttered with laughter, but Cheng stared at her in horror.

He pinched his tube shut. "Roshni! Your drink's escaping!"

Balls of orange liquid were shooting up into the air like bubbles, all in different directions.

"Oh no!" cried Roshni. "If we don't catch them, they'll get into the Beagle and stop it working properly! We'll crash!"

Chapter Six
BUGGY RIDE

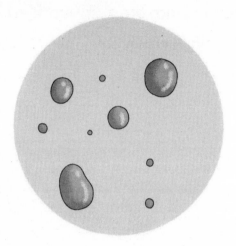

When Roshni saw Cheng try to catch the orange balls in his hands, she cried, "Stop! They'll splatter if you do that!"

Cheng grinned. "I'll catch them in my mouth, then!"

"Me, too!" said Roshni, stowing the pouches away. She had fun kicking off from the floor and trapping the orangey liquid in her mouth.

In spite of the danger of even one of the balls getting into the equipment, she couldn't help giggling when they bumped into each other and bounced off in different directions.

Cheng laughed as Roshni went after a ball, opening and closing her mouth and only catching it on her third try. "There's a goldfish in our pond that looks just like you," he said, as an orange ball drifted by his face. He opened his mouth and trapped it.

Roshni laughed. "And you look like a codfish!"

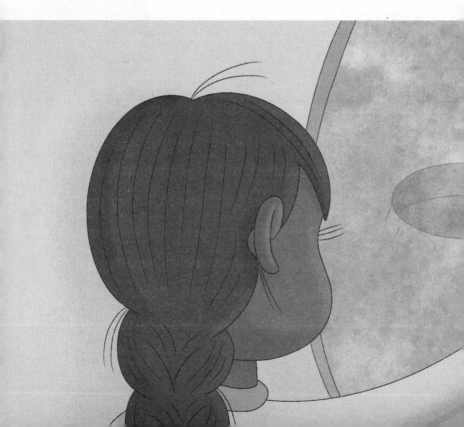

As Cheng caught the last liquid ball, Roshni noticed a glow of light shining through the window. "It's dawn!" she cried. "Dawn on the far side of the moon!"

"And the Beagle's landing," said Cheng. "Time to put our space suits back on."

Roshni grinned. "I hope you took your rocks out of my backpack," she said.

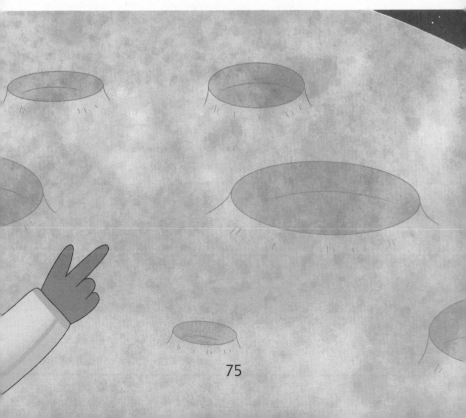

"Oops! Doing it now," said Cheng.

The Beagle landed so gently that they barely realized it had happened. When they were ready, they gave each other a thumbs-up, and Roshni led the way down the ladder to the moon's surface.

"Even though we know roughly where the lunar rover's trapped," said Cheng, "it's going to take us forever to search even a small area."

Roshni stood by a large panel in the underside of the Beagle. "I have a surprise," she said. "At least, I hope I do."

She opened the panel, releasing an odd-looking piece of machinery. It unfolded itself and when it rolled out on to the dusty surface, Cheng stared at it. Roshni watched his face light up as he realized what it was.

"A moon buggy!" he cried. "It looks a bit

like the Beagle does when it comes up through the floor in the Exploration Station! But a lot smarter!"

Roshni noticed writing on the side of the buggy. "Look, it's called 'Katherine'. It must be named after Katherine Johnson."

"Who's she?" asked Cheng, climbing into one of the buggy's seats.

"She was a brilliant mathematician. She used geometry to figure out the flight paths to get the first astronauts to the moon," said Roshni. She got into the driver's seat. "Come on, Katherine," she said. "Help us find that lunar rover!"

She sat for a moment. "Aren't you going to make it go?" Cheng asked.

Roshni paused. "I don't know how," she admitted.

Cheng pointed to a T-shaped controller. "Maybe if you push that forward we'll go forward, and if you push it right..."

Roshni grinned. "Okay, I've got it, thanks."

She eased the controller forward and the buggy jerked and bumped its way across the ground. "We're off—yay!" she cheered.

As they traveled, Roshni steered them around the rocks while Cheng kept a lookout for any sign of the lost lunar rover.

It was a weird, bumpy journey. Roshni was almost mesmerized by the gray scene before her. She glanced at Cheng, who was craning his neck to scan their surroundings.

"Can you believe we're driving on the moon?" Roshni asked, her voice wobbling as they boomp-boomp-boomped over small rocks and stones.

He shook his head. "Every so often I want

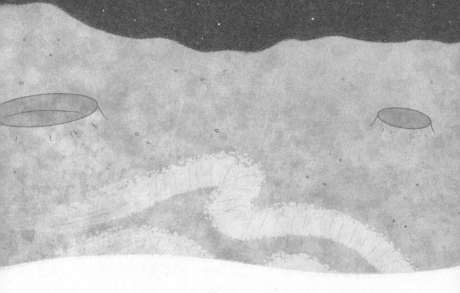

to pinch myself so I know I'm not dreaming, but it's impossible to do that through this thick... What's that?" He leaned forward, pointing. "Tracks! I'm sure those are tire tracks!"

"Wow! Eagle eyes," said Roshni, steering in the direction he pointed. She soon realized Cheng was right. "Those must be the lost rover's tracks."

"Fantastic!" said Cheng.

They followed the tracks toward a slight rise just ahead.

"That looks like the edge of a crater," said Cheng.

Roshni slowed the buggy as they approached it. It was like a wall with a rugged side that sloped down toward them. Just before the edge, she pulled up, and they climbed out. Roshni was so excited at finding the tracks that she'd forgotten how different it was walking on the moon, and almost tumbled over. She fell slowly, and Cheng grabbed her before she hit the ground.

"Thanks," she said. "For a moment, I was scared I might rip my suit."

"Yeek!" said Cheng. "That would be a disaster. If all your air escaped..."

Roshni broke in hastily. "Let's not think about it," she said. "Let's just be careful."

They climbed up the crater's sloping wall so they could peer over the edge. There, below them, in the dusty, bowl-shaped crater was the lunar rover!

They'd found it. They could complete their mission!

Roshni looked at the rover's situation. "It must have tumbled into the crater," she said, "and the sides are too steep for it to climb out."

"It's odd that it's stopped," said Cheng. "Isn't it supposed to keep going?"

"It should," said Roshni. "It runs on solar power, and there's no shortage of sunlight here. I'll check it when it's out of the crater."

Cheng looked doubtful. "Roshni, even if we can get it going," he said, "we still have a problem. It can't climb those steep sides by itself."

Roshni frowned. "But if it can't," she said, "how can we rescue it?"

Cheng groaned. "Don't tell me that, after all our traveling, our mission's going to fail?"

Roshni was very upset. "I'm afraid it might." She slid back down the crater wall and started toward the buggy. *Our mission will not fail,* she thought. *I won't let the Secret Explorers down. I'll figure out a solution—somehow.*

Chapter Seven
IN THE CRATER

Roshni clambered all over the buggy, looking for anything that might help them rescue the rover. She checked under the seats, behind them, in little compartments—there was nothing of any use. Finally, she walked around the outside and saw a panel at the back that she hadn't noticed before. It had a handle. She pulled it open.

"I've got something!" she yelled.

"Ow! Don't shout when you're wearing your helmet," said Cheng. "You nearly blew my ears out!"

"Sorry," she said. "I forgot you hear my voice so close to your ears. I'm excited because I've found a winch at the back of the buggy. We can use it to pull the rover out of the crater!"

"Awesome," said Cheng. He kangaroo-hopped to the driver's side and checked that the brake was on. Then he helped Roshni unspool the winch's cable. Taking the end with the hook, he looped the cable around his waist, using the hook to secure it.

"That's a smart idea," said Roshni. "You'll still have your hands free to climb down to the rover."

They clambered over the crater's edge. "I wish we didn't have space suits on," said Roshni. "This would be an easy climb on Earth."

She had no difficulty finding footholds, but they were small and her space boots were bulky. She glanced across at Cheng, who was making better progress. Of course! *Geologists must climb all the time*, she thought. "Cheng!" she called. "I'm worried that these little ledges won't hold my weight. Are they likely to crumble?"

Cheng peered carefully at the rocks. "It's fine," he assured her. "These are igneous rocks. They were formed from molten rock that cooled and set hard. Granite's an igneous rock and I know how hard that is—I once bumped my head on a granite floor!"

Roshni breathed a sigh of relief. "I'm so glad the Exploration Station chose you for this mission," she said. "And I'm really glad this crater's quite a shallow one," she added, looking down over her shoulder.

They were nearly at the crater floor when Cheng spoke again. "Be careful of the dust," he said. "Remember you told me there's no wind here? Without wind to erode the dust particles and smooth them off, they'll probably have very sharp edges."

"That's not really a problem while we're wearing space suits," said Roshni.

Cheng snorted. "It would be if it cut through your suit," he warned.

Just as he said that, Roshni knocked her knee on a rock. "Ouch!" she said, then caught her breath. "Cheng!" she cried in panic. "I bashed my knee. Is my suit okay? Can you see? Is it torn?" She felt sick with fear.

He clambered sideways. "It looks fine," he said. "There's just a gray scrape mark. I'll just check that the rock's not damaged."

That made Roshni laugh, but her heart was still thumping. Then she remembered that space suits were designed to protect astronauts from tiny meteorites and from extreme heat or cold. Of course it would survive a knock.

She reached the bottom of the crater just after Cheng, and they made their way to the lunar rover. It was smaller than their buggy.

Roshni looked around it to see if she could figure out why it had stopped roving. There didn't seem to be any damage—it was just very dusty.

"I guess that dust was thrown up when the rover fell into the crater, and it slowly settled back down all over it," said Cheng.

Roshni stared at him. "You are brilliant!" she said.

He stared back. "Huh?"

"You've given me the answer without realizing it." Roshni pointed out the rover's solar panels. "Look! They're covered in dust. The rover's not receiving enough sunlight to power it. That's what's wrong."

"Yay! Then let's get it out of here so it can charge up and be on its way," said Cheng. He attached the cable hook to the front of the rover. "I'll climb back up and handle the winch," he said.

"Okay," said Roshni. While she waited, she leaned against the rover and looked up at the stars. They were in different places from when she looked through her telescope at home. *I'm so lucky*, she thought, *to see things hardly any humans have seen.*

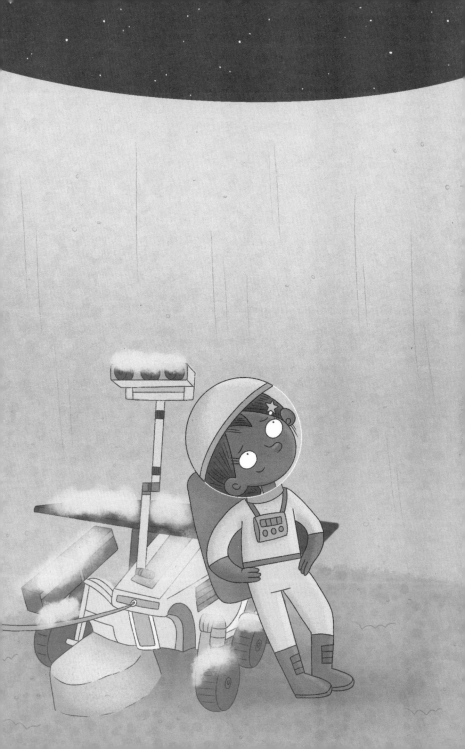

The rover jerked, making her jump. Cheng had started the buggy.

The winch cable dragged the rover across the crater floor—right into a wide, flat-topped boulder!

"Stop, Cheng!" she called, thankful for their suits' communication system. "There's a huge rock in the way. The winch can't possibly pull the rover over it."

Her heart sank. They'd been so sure of success. Was the mission going to end right there? It certainly looked like it.

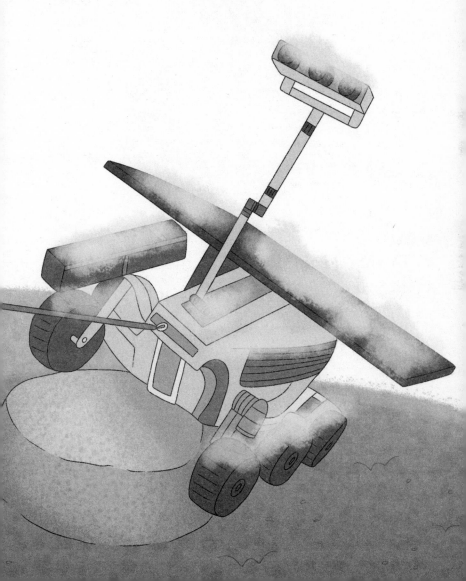

Chapter Eight
DUSTING

Cheng looked down from the crater's edge. Roshni held out her arms, as if to say, "Now what?" She thought of all they'd achieved to get this far, even mending the Beagle's...

Wait a minute! she thought, remembering how light the rock that Cheng put in her backpack had felt. *What was the fact she'd learned from one of her astronomy books?*

Since the moon's gravity is one-sixth of Earth's gravity, an astronaut would find that an object on the moon seems six times lighter than it would on Earth.

"Cheng!" she shrieked.

"Roshni! My ears!" came the frantic reply.

"Sorry," she said. "But watch this."

She reached out, got a firm grip on the back of the rover, and lifted it.

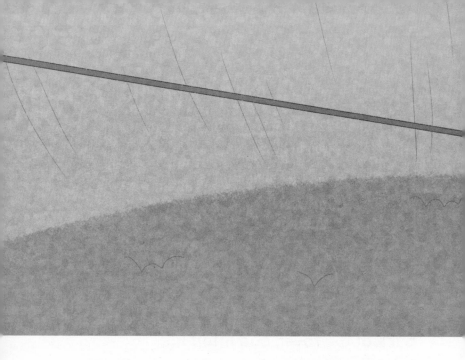

Cheng gave a long, low, "Woooowww!"

"Aren't I amazing?" she laughed. "The boulder's not very tall and it's flat on top—I can help the rover over!" She giggled. It was such a simple solution to a difficult problem.

Cheng laughed, too. "I'll agree you're amazing if you can lift something that big back on Earth! I'll start the buggy. Stand by!"

As the winch tugged at the rover, Roshni lifted the front end on to the

boulder. Then she went to the back, lifted and pushed. The rover rolled across the top and down the other side, landing with a thump. Roshni's heart was in her mouth. Was it damaged?

But the winch pulled the rover slowly to the crater wall and began to drag it up the side. Roshni started climbing, too. Luckily, climbing was easy in low gravity. She felt she could almost leap up!

By the time she joined Cheng, he'd unhooked the winch from the rover. Roshni opened the buggy's tool compartment and found exactly what she needed—a small hand brush.

"That's like the one I found," said Cheng. "It's probably for brushing dust off rock samples," he added. "I'll clean my rocks with it when we get back to the Beagle."

Roshni was horrified. "You're not brushing dust inside a space craft," she said. "Remember the drink mix?!"

Cheng grinned. "Just joking!" he said. "What's it for, anyway?"

Roshni grinned. "To sweep the dust off the rover's solar panels," she said. "Then the sunlight can charge them."

The dust sparkled as she brushed it. She worked quickly and, when she'd finished, she backed away from the particles that floated around her. "We shouldn't carry any dust back to the Beagle on our suits," she said as she put the brush away.

They sat in the buggy for a short rest. Roshni was quiet. It had been nighttime when she left New Delhi. *I'll close my eyes, just for a minute*, she thought...

She opened them with a jerk, and wondered if she'd actually fallen asleep. Cheng was shaking her shoulder. "Look!" he said. "The rover's wobbling! It must be falling to pieces."

"Oh no!" she cried. They kangaroo-hopped over to see.

Roshni grinned. "You know why it's wobbling, Cheng? It's starting up! The solar panels are working!"

They jumped for joy. Roshni squealed with delight at how high she went.

A few moments later, the rover rolled forward.

"Hooray!" they cheered. Then they both said, "Don't shout!" and laughed.

"There it goes," said Roshni, as the rover trundled away. "It's heading to the far side of the moon. Good luck!"

Once Cheng and Roshni were back on board the Beagle, Cheng asked, "Can we find out which crater that was?"

"Yes, let's do that," said Roshni. She brought the moon map up on the screen, and scrolled until it showed the far side. There were far more craters than on the side that faced Earth, and many of them were named.

A pulsing light showed the Beagle's location. Roshni traced the direction they'd taken in the buggy until she put her finger on the crater where the rover was stuck.

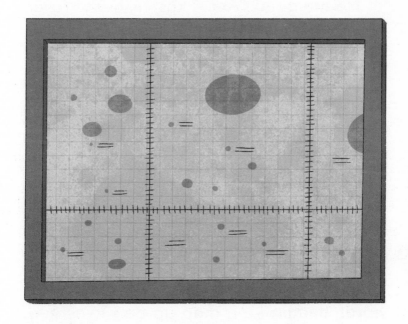

Cheng leaned over. "Is that it?"

Roshni gave a small nod.

"That's a shame," said Cheng. "It doesn't have a name."

"I know," Roshni said. Her voice shook.

Cheng looked at her. "What's wrong?"

"Nothing," she said. "It's—it's just amazing. The crater hasn't been named."

He shrugged. "And?"

"Don't you see? It's our discovery. We went there. We can name it."

Cheng grinned. "Oh yes! Let's name it after the Secret Explorers! Connor-Tamiko-Leah-Kiki-"

Roshni laughed. "That's too long. Let's call it... Beagle Crater!"

"Perfect!" said Cheng. "And look!" On the map, beside their crater, was the word, "Beagle"!

BEEEPBIBIBEEPBEEP BEEP BEEP!

They laughed. "The Beagle's happy," said Roshni, "and we're happy because..."

"Mission accomplished!" they shouted. "Hooray!"

Clearly the Beagle knew it was time to

leave, because a seat belt sign flashed on.

Cheng and Roshni lay on their couches and strapped themselves in as they lifted off.

Roshni took a last look at the moon's surface. She felt sad to be leaving space, but she knew how lucky she was to have had such a wonderful experience. *It was more amazing than I could ever have dreamed*, she thought.

The Beagle rose and rose, then with a final *BEEP!* It accelerated into brilliant, dazzling white light.

Roshni's couch moved so she was sitting upright. *The Beagle's begun its transformation*, she thought. Her elbows touched the sides as it closed in around her and Cheng. They were sitting in the old go-kart once more. The white light faded, and they were back in the Exploration Station.

The other Secret Explorers crowded around.

"Congratulations!" Kiki and Connor said together.

Gustavo patted them on their backs. "An awesome mission!" he said.

"You were both amazing!" Leah added.

"I can't believe you were actually on the moon!" said Ollie. "How was it?"

Roshni and Cheng grinned at each other. "Out of this world!" they said.

Cheng brought out his two rocks. "Look what I brought back for our display shelves."

"Wow!" said Tamiko. "Are they moon rocks?"

"Yes, the one with little holes in it is called basalt," said Roshni, "and the other is breccia." She glanced at Cheng. "I had a great geologist with me!"

"And I had a brilliant astronomer with me!" said Cheng.

BEEP!

Everyone laughed.

"I think the Beagle already knows how smart it is," said Connor.

It was time to go home. The Secret Explorers all hoped they would soon be called for another mission.

"Bye, Cheng," Roshni said. "Bye, everyone. See you soon!"

She stepped back through the glowing door and found herself in the warm night air of her New Delhi garden. As always, no time had passed at home while she was away.

"Meow!" Luna jumped down from the mango tree. Roshni stroked her and returned to her telescope. She looked up at the night sky twinkling above, knowing that it held millions of secrets, just waiting to be discovered.

Roshni added Beagle Crater to her own moon map and wrote inside it a tiny R and C, for Roshni and Cheng. She paused, then added a B, and giggled as the striped cat jumped onto the map. "The Beagle was part of our mission," she said. "It deserves to be there, but I don't think you do, Luna!" she added, lifting her down.

Roshni looked up at the moon. It was full and bright. "I'll never, ever forget," she murmured to herself, "that I stood on the moon and looked at the stars—and our beautiful planet Earth."

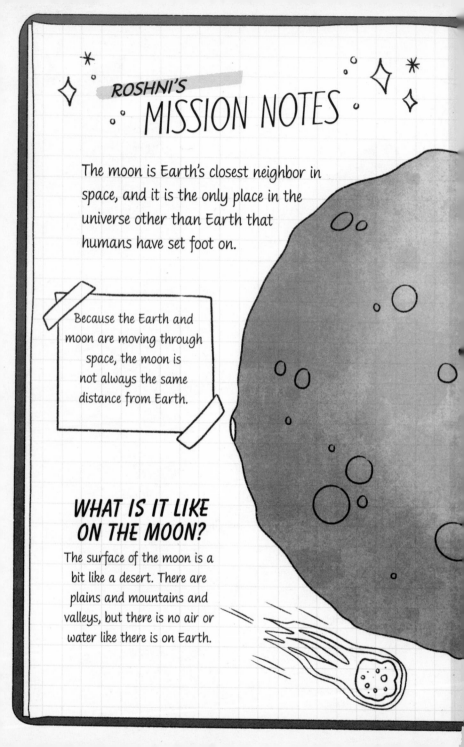

MISSION NOTES

The moon is Earth's closest neighbor in space, and it is the only place in the universe other than Earth that humans have set foot on.

Because the Earth and moon are moving through space, the moon is not always the same distance from Earth.

WHAT IS IT LIKE ON THE MOON?

The surface of the moon is a bit like a desert. There are plains and mountains and valleys, but there is no air or water like there is on Earth.

FACT FILE

* AGE: 4.5 billion years
* AVERAGE DISTANCE FROM EARTH: 238,900 miles (384,400km)
* TEMPERATURE ON THE SURFACE: -243°F (-153°C) to 253°F (123°C)
* TIME TO ORBIT THE EARTH: 27.3 days

WALKING ON THE MOON

Only 12 astronauts have ever walked on the moon's surface. The first people to walk on the moon were the American astronauts Neil Armstrong and Buzz Aldrin.

HOW THE MOON WAS FORMED

Scientists think the moon was formed around 4.5 billion years ago, when a planet called Theia crashed into the Earth.

At the time, Earth was still forming, and had stronger gravity than it does today.

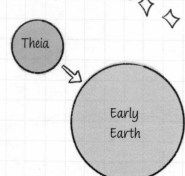

Theia

Early Earth

Theia is pulled to Earth

Around 4.5 billion years ago, Earth's gravity pulled Theia, which was a planet about the size of Mars, toward it at staggering speed.

Deep impact

When Theia crashed into Earth, pieces of rock and metal from both planets melted and mixed together. The force also knocked rocky materials into space.

The moon continues to orbit (move around) the Earth following the path of the rocky ring.

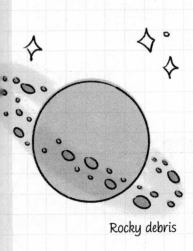

Rocky debris

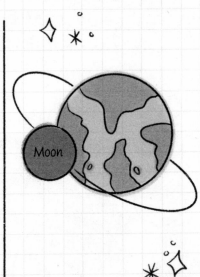

Moon

Forming a ring

Earth's gravity pulled the rocky material into a ring around it, while heavy materials (eg, iron and nickel) from both planets began to form the Earth's core.

Becoming the moon

Over time, the rocky material was pulled together by gravity into a lump. Eventually it cooled and formed into the moon as we know it today.

PHASES OF THE MOON

If you look at the sky on different nights of the month, it appears to change shape. These shapes are known as the "phases" of the moon, or the Lunar Cycle.

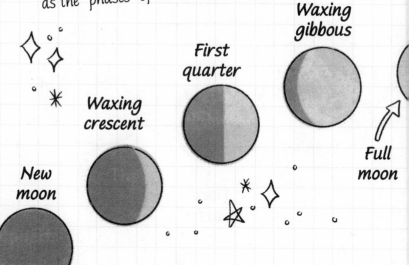

New moon

Waxing crescent

First quarter

Waxing gibbous

Full moon

≡ THE LUNAR CYCLE ≡

The different shapes of the moon we see are called phases. It takes 29.5 days for the moon to go through these phases. As the moon appears to grow, it is said to be "waxing" and as it appears to shrink it is "waning."

WHY DOES THE MOON APPEAR TO CHANGE SHAPE?

The moon doesn't create its own light. What we see when we look at it is a reflection of light from the sun lighting one side of the moon. As the moon orbits the Earth we see more or less of the lit side. The moon isn't actually changing shape, all that changes is the amount of the lit side we can see.

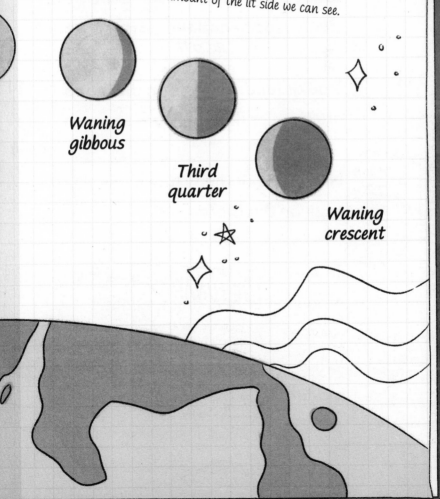

Waning gibbous

Third quarter

Waning crescent

QUIZ

1   What is the name for someone who studies space and the stars?

2   True or false: Objects on the moon are heavier than they are on Earth.

3   Name one of the first two people to walk on the Moon.

4   True or false: The dark side of the moon never gets any sunlight.

5   What was the name of the lunar module from the first moon landing?

6   True or false: The first moon landing took place in the year 1969.

7   How many years ago was the moon formed?

Check your answers on page 127

GLOSSARY

ASTRONAUT
Someone who is trained to travel and work in a spacecraft

ASTRONOMER
A scientist who studies stars, planets, and space

CRATER
A bowl-shaped dent on a planet or other body in space

FULL MOON
When the moon is fully illuminated in the night sky when viewed from Earth

FAR SIDE OF THE MOON
The part of the moon that always faces away from Earth

GRAVITY
A force that pulls objects together. The Earth's gravity keeps us on the ground

LIGHT POLLUTION

When lights from a city or other human-made source make it difficult to see the night sky

LUNAR APOGEE

The point during the moon's orbit of the Earth when it is farthest away

LUNAR MODULE

A small craft used to travel between a spacecraft and the surface of the moon

MOON

An object made of rock or rock and ice that orbits a planet or asteroid

ORBIT

The path of an object around a star, planet, or moon

ROVER

A vehicle that is driven on the surface of a planet or moon

SOLAR SYSTEM
The system of planets and other objects orbiting the sun

SPACESUIT
A suit worn by astronauts that allows them to survive in space

TELESCOPE
A tool that allows people to see faraway objects

Quiz answers

1. An astronomer

2. False

3. Neil Armstrong or Buzz Aldrin

4. False

5. The Eagle

6. True

7. 4.5 billion

DK | Penguin Random House

FSC MIX Paper from responsible sources FSC™ C018179

For Lily and Rhys

Text for DK by Working Partners Ltd
9 Kingsway, London WC2B 6XF
With special thanks to Valerie Wilding

Design by Collaborate Ltd
Illustrator Ellie O'Shea
Consultant Anita Ganeri

Acquisitions Editor James Mitchem
Designer Sonny Flynn
US Senior Editor Shannon Beatty
Publishing Coordinator Issy Walsh
Senior Production Editor Nikoleta Parasaki
Production Controller Francesca Sturiale
Publishing Director Sarah Larter

First American Edition, 2022
Published in the United States by DK Publishing
1450 Broadway, Suite 801, New York, New York 10018

A catalog record for this book is available
from the Library of Congress.
ISBN: 978-0-7440-4992-3 (paperback)
ISBN: 978-0-7440-4993-0 (hardcover)

DK books are available at special discounts when purchased in bulk
for sales promotions, premiums, fund-raising, or educational use.
For details, contact: DK Publishing Special Markets, 1450 Broadway,
Suite 801, New York, New York 10018
SpecialSales@dk.com

Printed and bound in Great Britain by
Clays Ltd, Elcograf S.p.A.

www.dk.com

For the curious